On His Bike!

Written by
Shirley Hughes

Illustrated by
Clara Vulliamy

RED FOX

for Tom with love from Shirley and Clara

Contents

Chapter One 1

Chapter Two 15

Chapter Three 29

Chapter Four 39

Chapter Five 59

Chapter Six 77

Chapter Seven 95

. . . and lots more for you to find!

MEET DIXIE and PERCY!

Dixie and his best friend, Percy, are always ready for adventure! They love to go off in Dixie's car, but we wanted to know what other things they like to do together, and all about their friendship. Let's see what they have to say . . .

Dixie and Percy, hello! Could you tell us about your perfect day out?

DIXIE: *For me, it's an energetic country walk, with plenty of hills to climb and streams with stepping stones to cross.*

PERCY: *And for me, after we've gone for a walk we can have a nice relaxing drive over to the Bella Vista Tearooms. Their cucumber sandwiches are the best for miles around.*

That sounds quite energetic, but how else do you like to keep fit?

PERCY: *Well, we have started a fitness routine, meeting up in the mornings to do our exercises.*

DIXIE: *I make sure I close the curtains though, in case Lou Ella is walking past . . .*

We know there are lots of things you enjoy doing together, but do you have any special skills?

DIXIE: *I am quite good at building model railways; they are all in the attic somewhere . . . but let me tell you about Percy – he is magnificent at ballroom dancing!*

PERCY: *Thank you, Dixie! I am very proud of my trophies.* **You two are such magnificient friends: what qualities do you think are important in a friend?**

DIXIE: *I think cheerful optimism and always being ready for a new adventure together.*

PERCY: *And for me it's loyalty – to be there for each other through thick and thin.* **And finally, I'm not sure we need to ask, but who is your best friend?**

PERCY: *Dixie!*

DIXIE: *Percy!*

Of course! Thank you so much, Dixie and Percy!

Lou Ella
likes:
Fast cars
New frocks
Feeling the wind
in her hair

Dean Delaney
likes:
Bikes
Races
Brand-new cycling clothes

Beryl Boothroyd
likes:
Lifting heavy boxes

Don Barrakan
likes:
Designing new bicycles

Arthur MacArthur
likes:
Being outdoors

N
W
E
S
DIDSWORTH CANAL
TOWPATH
UPPER DIDDLESWORTH
UPPER DIDDLESWORTH
THE BELLA VISTA TEAROOMS
DIDDLESWORTH LAKE
LOWER DIDDLESWORTH
DIDDLESWORTH BOG

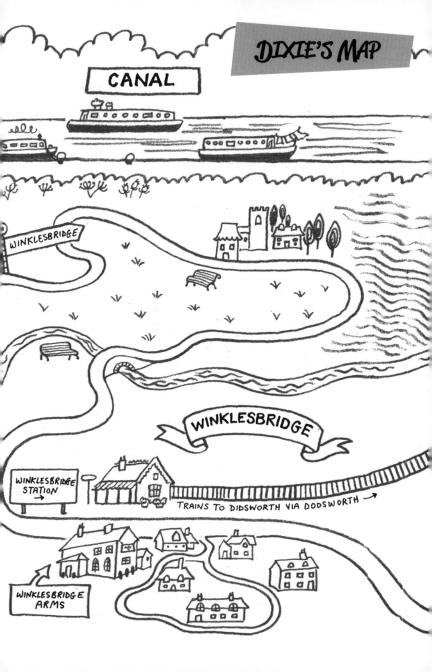

Chapter One

DIXIE O'DAY

One fine morning, when Dixie O'Day's friend Percy had come over to help him wash his car, a cyclist passed by.

He slowed down, dismounted, and stood watching them for a while. Then he said, in a friendly way:

'That's a lovely vehicle you have there. And you keep it in very good condition, I see.'

Dixie was pleased. He stood back, sponge in hand, to admire the sparkle on the windscreen.

'Thanks', he said. 'She's not the latest model exactly, but she goes beautifully. Never any trouble with the engine. Well, hardly ever. But I see you are a cyclist yourself.'

DIXIE O'DAY

'Yes – I love it. Go off on lots of long rides at weekends. I'm staying here in Didsworth with my auntie at the moment. Exploring the area a bit on my bike.'

'I'm Dixie and this is my friend Percy,' said Dixie. 'We were just thinking of having a coffee break. Would you care for a cup?'

On His Bike!

The cyclist introduced himself as Dean Delaney, and soon he and Dixie were chatting affably, discussing the merits of cycling versus motoring, while Percy put the final touches to the bumper of Dixie's car.

DIXIE O'DAY

'Look here,' said Dixie. 'I wonder if you'd care to join us sometime on a little trip around Didsworth in my car? I can see that you're a born cyclist, but perhaps we could take you further afield? There are some very picturesque views in the area.'

'Thanks, that's very kind of you,' Dean said, 'but I prefer to stick with my bike. It's far better exercise. Driving is all very well for older people, but it doesn't keep you fit, does it?'

And with that he was off, leaving Dixie and Percy staring at his disappearing form.

On His Bike!

After this Dixie
and Percy often
caught sight
of Dean

speeding down
the road,

off on some
new adventure.

DiXiE O'DAY

One morning, when Percy dropped
in on Dixie to see if they might plan
another car outing soon, he found
Dixie in his shorts, doing exercises.

'That looks very energetic!' he said.
'Well done, old chap!'

Dixie paused, panting. He was very
red in the face.

'Do you know, Percy,' he said,
'I think I may have put on a bit of
weight recently. My waistline seems to
have increased, and I can't do up the
bottom button of my waistcoat. I've
decided something has to be done.'

DiXiE O'DAY

'You could go on a diet,' Percy
suggested. 'And cut out all those
afternoon teas we've been having
recently at the Cottage Creamery.'

'Hmm. Yes. But I don't think that's enough. I think Dean is right. Driving everywhere in the car means I'm not getting enough exercise. As a matter of fact, I'm thinking of taking up cycling.'

Percy was amazed.

'But you haven't ridden a bicycle in years!' he said. 'Your old one is in the shed with flat tyres.'

DiXiE O'DAY

'I know. But I'm going to invest
in a new one. Something really
up to date. And – well, Percy, I'm
wondering if it should be a tandem!'

Chapter Two

DiXiE O'DAY

Percy couldn't understand Dixie's bold new plan of cycling on a tandem.

'You mean we should take to the road together, Dixie? But how could we do that? My legs would be too short to reach the pedals!' he exclaimed, in sheer astonishment.

But it turned out that Dixie had a cunning plan. He had been talking to his friend Don Barrakan, who was very interested in bicycles.

On His Bike!

Don had offered to design and make a special tandem which could be adapted so that he and Percy could ride it together.

DIXIE O'DAY

'I will be in front and you behind,' said Dixie. 'Think how fit we'll be!'

Percy was doubtful. He thought it might be a bit too strenuous to have to pedal behind Dixie and keep up with his pace.

GO FOR IT! ☆

But after many long phonecalls and trips over to Don's repair shop, the day arrived at last when the tandem was finally delivered, along with two very smart helmets.

On His Bike!

'Isn't this splendid, Percy!' exclaimed Dixie. 'Soon we'll be off – freewheeling across the countryside!

'We'll be wearing shorts, of course, and the latest thing in cycling clothes – the best that money can buy. Come on, Percy! Be a sport, and give it a try!'

DIXIE O'DAY

Dixie's enthusiasm was infectious, and Percy began to feel much braver. He climbed on the back of the shiny new bike.

'It's all coming back to me, Dixie! Perhaps this bicycling lark is for me, after all!'

On His Bike!

They pushed off down the
road. But they had not gone
far when, with a wobble
and a crash . . .

. . . the tandem toppled over,
bringing Dixie and Percy
down in a tangled heap.

DIXIE O'DAY

'Would you like some stabilizers, Percy?' asked Dixie, as he helped his friend to his feet. 'This may take a bit of practice at first.'

On His Bike!

So it was that Dixie and Percy began to be seen about Didsworth on the new adapted tandem, Dixie panting a little in front and Percy pedalling gamely along behind.

CHIPS AHOY!

DIDSWORTH TIDDLERS
Children's clothes and toys

DIXIE O'DAY

Naturally, Dean took a great interest in this new development.

'I'm glad I've convinced you that bicycling is best!' he said. 'Let's join forces and go for a trip together. I'll adapt my speed to yours, of course.'

So the plan went ahead. Dean came over to Dixie's house and they spent a great deal of time poring over the map together.

On His Bike!

Percy looked on. He did not
mention that he had brought his own
map, with a route carefully worked
out to take in many of the lovely
out-of-the-way places he and
Dixie had discovered together.
Now he quietly took it
out of his pocket and
sat on it.

Dixie did not notice
Percy's dejected face
as Dean pointed out all
the advantages of his
route – the beautiful views,
steep hills and byways which
he wanted them to explore.

DIXIE O'DAY

Once Percy tried to suggest that they could end their ride at one of his favourite places, the Bella Vista Tearooms in Upper Diddlesworth. But Dean loudly rejected the idea.

Dixie agreed. 'We can go there any time, Percy,' he said. 'It's good to try somewhere new.'

On His Bike!

After that, poor Percy sat quietly,
daydreaming of the trip he would
like to have planned.

DIXIE O'DAY

At night he lay awake, slightly dreading the upcoming trip, and thinking about their new friend. He was keen to see the best in Dean – after all, Dixie thought very highly of him.

Chapter Three

DIXIE O'DAY

Finally the day of their cycling expedition arrived. The three set off on their chosen route, but unfortunately, the road soon began to dwindle into a winding lane with high hedgerows, and then into a rough track. It was very heavy going.

'Shall we turn back soon?' Dixie called out, panting heavily. 'This doesn't look as though it's going to lead anywhere much.'

But to their dismay, it *was* leading somewhere, and that was towards a steep incline. Their bicycles gathered speed alarmingly, and soon they were tearing downhill at full tilt, bumping, swerving to avoid deep ruts, and jamming on their brakes until at last . . .

32

. . . both bicycles went straight into a haystack, hitting it full on.

They lay there for a while, wheels
spinning, their mouths full of hay.

On His Bike!

'Are you all right, Percy?' said Dixie at last in a muffled voice.

He was relieved to hear a faint answering squeak: 'Yes, I think so!'

'What about you, Dean?'

Dean cleared his throat. 'Yes, of course. You have to expect these spills now and again.'

It took them some time to extricate themselves and their bicycles, and get back up the track to a place where it was possible to remount.

'Shall we press on?' said Dean casually.

'No, I don't think so,' said Dixie. 'I think Percy and I have had enough for one day.'

When they had parted with Dean
and arrived back at Dixie's house,
their nosy neighbour Lou Ella was
lurking by her front gate as usual.
She always managed to be there when
some disaster or other had struck.

'You're back early!' she said.
'Finding all that cycling a bit
strenuous, I expect. Why are you
both covered in hay?'

DIXIE O'DAY

'Just a small mishap,' said Dixie as, with as much dignity as they could muster, he and Percy pushed the tandem round to the back of his house.

Chapter Four

This disaster did not put Dean off for long. He was back the following weekend with another expedition planned.

On His Bike!

This time he chose to leave
Didsworth on the winding
side road which led out of
town, past the children's playground
and on up towards the cliff top.
Dixie was quick to agree.

DiXiE O'DAY

This was a steep challenge, and it did not have happy memories for Percy as it reminded him of the occasion when he and Dixie nearly went over the edge of the cliff in Dixie's car.

DANGER
CLIFF
EDGE

But today all went well.
When they paused at
the top, Percy said:
'There are some beautiful
woods not far from
here. Perhaps we should
go there to eat our packed
lunches?'

But Dean was studying the map.

'I see there's a canal down there which looks interesting,' he said. 'Why don't we go and have a look at that first?'

On His Bike!

It took some time to find the path to the canal, but at last they found it; a narrow lane which led steeply down to the towpath.

Below, some barges were moored alongside the canal near the lock gates.

DiXiE O'DAY

'Let's freewheel down there and have a closer look at them,' said Dean.

'Is that wise?' Dixie replied, remembering their previous encounter with the haystack. 'Perhaps we should leave our bicycles up here and walk down?'

'Oh no! It'll be fun! Come on!' said Dean.

And he led the way
down the slope, gathering
speed very rapidly. Dixie and Percy
followed until they reached the
towpath.

DIXIE O'DAY

The towpath was narrow. Some of
the barges moored in the water were
proper little homes with neat curtains
and window boxes full of flowers.

On His Bike!

Delicious smells of cooking drifted up from the galley kitchens, which made Percy feel hungry. Some small children perched in the bows waved as they went past.

Then disaster struck. Dean, who was riding in front, came slap up against a van that was coming in the opposite direction.

FRESH
BREAD
baguettes

The driver pulled up sharply a few inches from Dean's front wheel.

On His Bike!

He wound down his cab window
and shouted angrily: 'What do you
think you're doing? It's my right
of way.'

DiXiE O'DAY

'Sorry!' said Dean. He tried to back his bicycle away, but somehow managed to hit Dixie's front wheel, causing the tandem to swerve sharply. Percy found himself hanging perilously over the side of the canal.

All the while the truck driver was inching forward, almost nudging Dean's front wheel with his bumper and eyeballing them furiously over his steering wheel.

DiXiE O'DAY

Meanwhile Percy was wobbling dangerously, poised right over the bow of one of the barges where the owner, Mrs Elsie Bywater, was hanging out her washing.

On His Bike!

Mrs Bywater shook her fist at him and shouted: 'How dare you? Your muddy back wheel is right over my home!'

'Terribly sorry, madam!' squeaked Percy. 'We didn't mean to intrude – just a small error of judgement. We'll be on our way in a moment!'

DIXIE O'DAY

Dixie edged the tandem forward
very cautiously; then, greatly to their
relief, managed to pull Percy's end
back onto the towpath.

On His Bike!

The truck was still bearing down on them. On this occasion even Dean decided to give up. They turned round and, with Dixie and Percy leading the way, wheeled their bicycles back up the hill.

'Pity,' said Dean. 'I'd like to have seen the lock gates.'

'Another time, perhaps,' said Dixie wearily.

Chapter Five

DIXIE O'DAY

It was not long before Dean dropped by
Dixie's house again.

'I do hope our little encounter with
the haystack and our spot of bother
on the towpath hasn't discouraged
you in your cycling plans,' he said.

On His Bike!

'Perhaps you'd care to take part in a long-distance race? Something really ambitious! And whoever loses will buy a slap-up tea at the other end.'

'Sounds like a grand idea,' Dixie replied enthusiastically.

'Oh dear,' said Percy after Dean had gone. 'This all sounds a bit strenuous.'

DIXIE O'DAY

But the plan went ahead.

Dixie and Dean spent a great deal of time consulting road maps. It was to be an all-day affair.

On His Bike!

'We'll do it in stages,' said Dean. 'I suggest we time ourselves at meeting points along the way. And whoever gets there first records their time and then waits for the other to catch up. That will give us all time for a breather and make it easier for you two.'

The HIDDEN GEMS of DIDSWORTH and surrounding areas

Map of special places

DIXIE O'DAY

'Sounds like a good idea,' said Dixie. Privately, Percy was doubtful. 'It's a very long way, Dixie,' he said.

'The final meeting place is way over in Winklesbridge! It will take the whole day – and then we've got to get back again. And what about provisions? We can't take a big picnic basket on the back of our bike.'

On His Bike!

'Don't worry, there's sure to be a café or two en route,' said Dixie reassuringly.

They set out at dawn. Luckily, the weather was fine.

Dean sped off ahead of them at record pace – so fast that by the time they reached the next corner they had lost sight of him altogether.

DiXiE O'DAY

When they arrived at the first
rendezvous, they found him sitting
at ease on a bench, sipping a cup of
coffee. He consulted his watch.

'Right – I make it eight forty-five,'
he said. 'I was here at ten past, so that
puts me thirty-five minutes in the lead.
Shall we press on?'

66

On His Bike!

Percy was dismayed. 'But what about our breather?' he asked.

'Oh, don't you think we should miss out on this one and make some progress before it gets too hot?' said Dean.

With that he shot off, and Dixie and Percy resolutely started pedalling again.

DiXiE O'DAY

As the day wore on, the journey got increasingly gruelling for Dixie and Percy. By lunch time they were less than halfway to Winklesbridge.

It had taken Dean
two hours
and ten minutes,

but Dixie and Percy had already clocked up three and a quarter hours.

On His Bike!

They were getting very tired, and, especially on the main roads, kept being overtaken by cars and trucks.

They never seemed to spot Dean, who immediately shot ahead, showing no signs of exhaustion.

And he was always at the next rendezvous

as fresh as a daisy.

DIXIE O'DAY

Dusk was falling when, at last, Dixie and Percy pulled in at the final meeting point, which was Winklesbridge Station. Dean was already there, chatting with the station master.

It was an outright win for Dean, of course, and Dixie and Percy were sporting enough to congratulate him warmly.

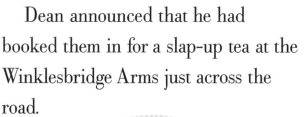

On His Bike!

Dean announced that he had booked them in for a slap-up tea at the Winklesbridge Arms just across the road.

It was indeed a very good tea, as it should have been, because it was very expensive. Poor Percy, who had looked forward to this part of the trip all day, was almost too tired to enjoy it.

DiXiE O'DAY

When they had finished and Dixie
had paid the bill, he said to the others:
'I'm afraid cycling back to
Didsworth is out of the question now.
So I think it would be better if we
took the train home, don't you?
We can pay to put our bicycles
in the guard's van.'

'That sounds like a good idea for you two,' said Dean. 'As it happens, I have an old school friend who lives near here, so my plan is to ask him to put me up for the night, and I'll cycle back tomorrow. I'd invite you two if I could, but I'm afraid there wouldn't be enough room for us all.'

DiXiE O'DAY

Dixie and Percy were both dismayed when they heard this. But there seemed to be nothing they could do except politely say goodbye to Dean and trudge back to the station.

The station master was just closing the ticket hatch.

On His Bike!

'Two singles to Didsworth, please,' said Dixie. 'And may we book our tandem into the guard's van?'

'Afraid not. The last train to Didsworth left an hour ago.'

Dixie closed his eyes. This was the last straw after a very tiring day.

DIXIE O'DAY

'The milk train will be through at five thirty tomorrow morning,' said the station master. 'You can sleep in the waiting room if you like.'

Chapter Six

DIXIE O'DAY

None of these misadventures, not even
a very uncomfortable night spent in
Winklesbridge Station waiting room,
had put Dixie off his cycling craze.
He was fired up with excitement when
it was announced that there was to be
a bicycle rally in Didsworth.

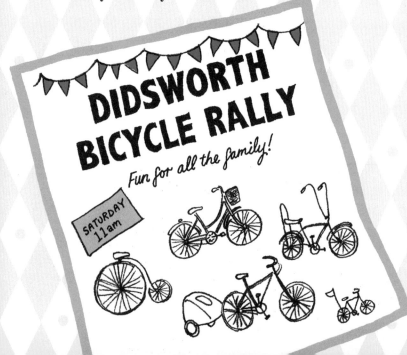

DIDSWORTH
BICYCLE RALLY
Fun for all the family!

SATURDAY
11am

On His Bike!

'We must enter this, of course!' Dixie said enthusiastically.

Percy sighed. 'What's the point? Dean's sure to win.'

'Oh, come on, Percy – this is not like you. Where's your competitive spirit?'

DIXIE O'DAY

But Percy's competitive spirit was in short supply; he had had enough of Dean and his challenges. He longed for the days when he and Dixie would stroll along to the Cottage Creamery, or tootle around in Dixie's car.

On His Bike!

The starting point for the race was outside Didsworth church. Lou Ella watched them set out. She had already made it quite clear that she despised cycling as an altogether inferior form of transport, and had no intention of being a spectator, let alone entering the race.

DIXIE O'DAY

When Dixie and Percy arrived,
they found all kinds of cyclists already
assembled at the start.

On His Bike!

There was a race for children, who were being given a special route of their own. The three little ones from the friendly family, who had come to Dixie and Percy's rescue once when they were in grave danger, were ready for the off.

Children's Race

Dean, of course, was entering the main race. He stood back coolly, waiting for the race to start.

DIXIE O'DAY

The watching crowds cheered as the starting flag for the main race went down, and they were away!

Dixie and Percy were pedalling as never before, but several competitors were already ahead of them, including Dean, who had pulled out almost immediately, clipping Dixie and Percy's wheel, and was forging ahead.

On His Bike!

As they surged towards the level crossing, it was becoming clear who were the strong competitors.

Don Barrakan was one, and Arthur MacArthur, a small wiry fellow who worked over at Pickwick Farm, was another.

DIXIE O'DAY

By the time they reached the level crossing, Arthur and Don were vying for the lead. Dean, in spite of a promising start, was now losing ground badly.

On His Bike!

Dixie and Percy were making
a gallant effort, and the spectators
lining the route yelled out friendly
encouragement to the two friends.

'You're doing brilliantly, Percy,'
shouted Dixie as Percy's legs spun so
fast you could hardly see them.

Percy's chest swelled with pride.

DIXIE O'DAY

Now, as the front runners Arthur
and Don were approaching the railway
bridge, another cyclist shot forwards
and began gaining on them fast.

On His Bike!

It was Beryl Boothroyd, who
worked for the local removal company,
Griff's Nifty Moves! She was riding
a very stylish, up-to-the-minute
machine. Her muscular legs seemed
to move effortlessly as she powered
determinedly towards the front.

DIXIE O'DAY

By the time they reached the level stretch of road by the old windmill, she was challenging Don and Arthur for the lead.

'Come on, Beryl! You can do it!'
the crowd shouted.

On His Bike!

Dean was now fighting for a place among a crowd of cyclists who were all striving to overtake each other. Beryl, Arthur and Don were out in front.

DIXIE O'DAY

But as they swung round the dangerous corner and into the long home stretch that led back into Didsworth, the front wheel of Don's bike hit a stone and he pitched forward onto the ground.

On His Bike!

A great gasp of sympathy went up from the crowd as two stewards ran out and helped him back on his bike.

Now, Beryl and Arthur were pedalling furiously, neck and neck, way out in front of all the others. They both looked exhausted, but the crowd was cheering them on.

DIXIE O'DAY

When at last they reached the finish and the flag went down, Beryl's front wheel was a fraction ahead of Arthur's. She had won the race!

Chapter Seven

DiXiE O'DAY

Arthur and Don, who had come in second and third place, came forward at once to congratulate her. Then the cheering crowd engulfed her, and she was carried away in triumph.

Dean finished much later, dismounted and walked away without a word.

On His Bike!

Dixie and Percy cycled slowly home, tired, but not downhearted.

'I'm sorry if I let you down,' said Percy.

'I think we did pretty well,' said Dixie. 'You were a wonderful sport, Percy. And I'd rather be last with you than first on my own.'

DIXIE O'DAY

'I'm glad we had a go,' said Percy. 'Dean didn't do as well as he'd expected, did he? Funny, that, considering how fast he was the other day, cycling to Winklesbridge in such record time.'

'I expect he'll turn up with another ambitious plan soon,' Dixie said.

But he was wrong. They never saw Dean again. To their surprise, some days later they heard that he had left Didsworth without saying goodbye to anyone.

DEAN DELANEY,
3 DAISY LANE,
DIDSWORTH

return to sender—
no longer at this
address

DIXIE O'DAY

One sunny morning, a week or
two after the excitement of the race
had died down, Dixie and Percy were
enjoying coffee and cake at their friend
Ron Barrakan's roadside diner. They
had decided to give the tandem a rest
for the time being, and had come out for
a leisurely drive in Dixie's car.

On His Bike!

A truck driver who had just filled up with petrol at Ron's garage strolled over, sipping his cup of tea.

'You're the chaps who ride the tandem, aren't you?' he said. 'I saw you and your friend on the road to Winklesbridge the other day.'

DIXIE O'DAY

'Yes – that's us. He challenged us to a long-distance bicycle race and won hands down.'

The driver took another sip.

'Oh yes. I remember him all right. As a matter of fact, I gave him and his bike a lift –or rather, several lifts – in the back of my truck.'

'A lift?' said Dixie.

'Oh yes. He thumbed a lift with his bike just outside Didsworth and stopped off at several places along the road to Winklesbridge while I made some local deliveries.'

'Well, I'm blowed!' Dixie exclaimed. 'So that's how he managed to get ahead of us all the time, and not be in the least bit tired! What a cheat! And to think we stood him a slap-up tea at the end of it!'

DIXIE O'DAY

That evening, when the two friends were chatting by the fire, Dixie said: 'I'm afraid that chap Dean was one of those people who can't bear not to win everything. Thoroughly unsporting! And I was completely taken in by him – put you through a lot of exhausting rides too, Percy. Perhaps we should give up the tandem altogether.'

'Oh no, Dixie,' Percy replied. 'I rather like it, as a matter of fact. I feel I'm just getting the hang of it. I love the car, of course. But let's do cycling too, for the joy of it – and who cares whether we win or lose!'

On His Bike!

'You're a true friend, Percy!' said
Dixie. 'And what's more, you're the
best map reader I've ever met!'

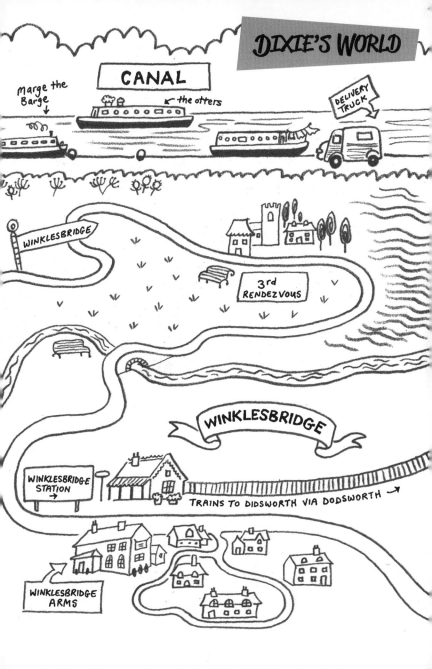

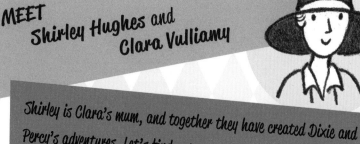

MEET
Shirley Hughes and Clara Vulliamy

Shirley is Clara's mum, and together they have created Dixie and Percy's adventures. Let's find out more about them!

Hello, Shirley and Clara!

Can you tell us what your perfect day out is?

Shirley: A stroll along the towpath, and supper with my grandchildren.

Clara: A day out with Mum on our brand-new tandem!

And how do you like to keep fit?

Shirley: I walk everywhere!

Clara: By running up and down the stairs looking for things I've forgotten or lost . . .

Can you tell us if you have any special skills?

Shirley: Writing, drawing and making my own clothes.

Clara: Writing, drawing and making chocolate puddings.

Very useful! Now, what qualities do you think are important in a friend?

Shirley: For me, it's good company and chatting about the old days.

Clara: And for me, it's being forgiving and kind, and telling funny stories.

Can you tell us if you have ever had an argument with a friend, and if so, how did you make up?

Shirley: I do my level best to avoid arguments!

Clara: Once, after an argument, me and my friend each wrote what was making us cross on a piece of paper, and without showing each other, crumpled them up and threw them in the fire! Then it was all forgotten and we felt much better.

That's a very good idea! Shirley and Clara, thank you for talking to us!

There are ten differences between these two pictures – can you spot them all? *(Answers on the next page.)*

Marvellous Maps!

Dixie and Percy are always heading off on adventure, with their trusty map to guide the way – Percy is an excellent map-reader!

DIDSWORTH

DIDSWORTH STATION

N
E
S

Can you make your own map?
It can show roads, rivers and train tracks, buildings, bridges – anything you think is important. It could be where you really live, or somewhere from your imagination . . .

When you've drawn your map, go to **www.dixieoday.com** to find out how to send your pictures to Dixie and Percy!

The Dixie O'Day Quiz

Dixie has written a special quiz to test you! How much can you remember about *Dixie O'Day: On His Bike?*

1. True or false: Dean Delaney rides a motorcycle.

2. What is the name of the special kind of bicycle for two that Dixie and Percy have made?

3. True or false: Dean, Dixie and Percy cycle to the Bella Vista Tearooms together.

4. What do Dean, Dixie and Percy crash into on their first outing?

5. True or false: Lou Ella loves cycling.

6. True or false: Dean falls into the canal.

7. What is Dean's prize for winning the race to Winklesbridge?

8. True or false: Dixie and Percy have to sleep in the station waiting room.

9. What is Beryl Boothroyd's job?

10. Who wins the bicycle rally?

11. True or false: Dean moves in next door to Dixie.

12. True or false: Dean cheated in the race to Winklesbridge.